For my son, Jack

First published 2006 by Macmillan Children's Books
a division of Macmillan Publishers Limited
20 New Wharf Road, London N1 9RR
Basingstoke and Oxford
Associated companies throughout the world
www.panmacmillan.com

ISBN-13: 978-1-4050-5061-6
ISBN-10: 1-4050-5061-6

Text and illustrations copyright
© Chris Riddell 2006

The right of Chris Riddell to be identified
as the author and illustrator of
this work has been asserted by
him in accordance with the
Copyright, Designs and
Patents Act 1988.

9 8 7 6 5 4 3 2 1

A CIP catalogue record for this book is
available from the British Library.

Printed in Belgium

The Emperor of Absurdia

Chris Riddell

Macmillan Children's Books

The Emperor of Absurdia was having
the most extraordinary dream.

All of a **sudden** he woke to the **hoots** of the sky fish nibbling the umbrella trees.

He tumbled

out of

bed . . .

. . . into the arms
of the
Wardrobe
Monster.

The Wardrobe Monster
helped the Emperor
get dressed —

in a
bobbly hat,

a crumply
coat,

and a pair of
jingle-jangle
socks.

"Have you seen my **snuggly scarf** anywhere?" the Emperor asked.

The Wardrobe Monster shook his big hairy head.

"That's funny, I had it yesterday," said the Emperor, and set off on a scarf hunt . . .

. . . which took quite some time.

"It's no good," said the Emperor, sitting under a pointy tree. "I can't find my snuggly scarf anywhere."

Just then, from the top of the tree, there came a loud, pointy-sounding **squawk.**

The Emperor climbed the pointy tree and found a pointy nest . . . and there was his **snuggly scarf.**

The Emperor of Absurdia put on his scarf and went to his high chair.

Breakfast was served.

And then supper,

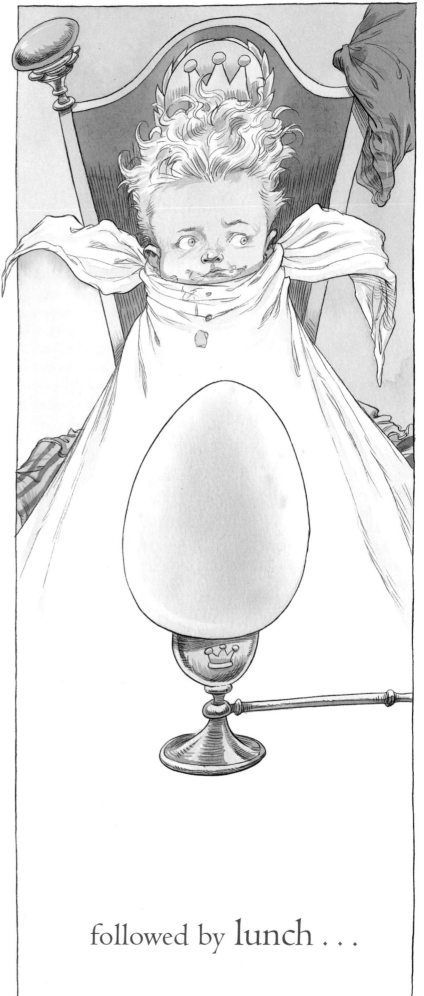

followed by lunch . . .

. . . which hatched . . .

and
flew
away.

"This is
exciting!"
said the Emperor.

The Emperor of Absurdia called for his
tricycle chair
and set
off on a
**dragon
hunt . . .**

. . . which took quite some time.

He looked
in the
flower beds
and up the
**umbrella
trees.**

He looked
under
the **pillow
hills**

and over the bouncy mountains.

"It's no good," said the Emperor,
climbing down from his tricycle chair.
"I can't find the little dragon
anywhere."

He was just about
to give up, when he
noticed the footprints.

They led into
a deep, dark
cave.

The Emperor took off his **bobbly hat** and his **jingle-jangle socks** and put them in the pocket of his **crumply coat**.

Then, as quietly as he could, he tiptoed inside the cave.

And
out
again!

"Help!" cried
the Emperor.
"An emperor hunt!"

The dragon chased the Emperor across the bouncy mountains

and through the pillow hills,

under the umbrella trees and towards the flower beds.

Then, just as
the dragon was
about to gobble
the Emperor up,
there came a loud,
pointy-sounding
squawk
and a pointy
bird swooped
down and
caught
hold of the
Emperor's
scarf.

As they **flew** over the flower beds,
the Emperor let go of the scarf
and **tumbled**
down through
the air . . .

into the
arms of
the Wardrobe
Monster.

He was
so pleased to
see the Emperor
that he gave him
an **extra**
big hug.

"I'll look
for my
snuggly scarf
tomorrow," said
the Emperor, and
the Wardrobe
Monster nodded
his big hairy head.

Then, as a big buttercup moon
rose in the sky, the Emperor of
Absurdia tumbled into bed
and fell fast asleep.

And as the sky fish snored
in the umbrella trees . . .

. . . he had
the most
extraordinary
dream.